The Right House for Rabbit

By Susan Saunders
Illustrated by Jody Lee

A GOLDEN BOOK • NEW YORK
Western Publishing Company, Inc., Racine, Wisconsin 53404

Rabbit was tired of his house. Every day he woke up in the same room. Every day he saw the same things outside his window.

"I'm tired of looking at that crooked old pine tree,"
Rabbit said to himself one morning. "I'm tired of that
round, brown hill. Today I'm going to find a new place
to live."

Rabbit brushed his ears and put on his best suit. Then he hopped into town to talk to Mr. Fox at the rental office.

FOX RENTALS

"So you're looking for a new house," said Mr. Fox. "I'm sure I have something you'll like."

"I want a house with a nice view," Rabbit told him.

"A view?" said Mr. Fox. "Let me see...." He opened a notebook and turned a few pages. "Here's just the thing," he said. "Go to the third house on Bird Lane. There's a red mailbox out front."

The red mailbox belonged to Mrs. Robin. "Are you renting your house?" Rabbit asked her.

"Yes, indeed," said Mrs. Robin. "My children have flown to homes of their own, and I'm moving south myself."

"Mr. Fox said you have a nice view," said Rabbit.

"A lovely view," said Mrs. Robin. "Come right up."

There was a wonderful view from Mrs. Robin's house. Stretched out in front of Rabbit were rivers and lakes and hills. In back of him lay all of the town.

But leaves blew into Rabbit's face. And acorns dropped down his collar. And twigs fell onto his head. "Where is your roof?" Rabbit asked Mrs. Robin.

Before Mrs. Robin could answer, a fuzzy yellow worm wriggled out of the tree. It crawled across Rabbit's sleeve.

Mrs. Robin fixed the worm with a greedy eye. Then she neatly pecked it off and swallowed it. "Who needs a roof?" she said. "A roof would just get in my way."

Rabbit wanted a roof over his head. He hopped back to Mr. Fox's office.

"Did you like the view?" asked Mr. Fox.

"Lovely," said Rabbit. "But my house must have a roof. And walls would be nice."

"A roof, and some walls." Mr. Fox looked in his notebook again. "Well, then," he said, "go to the lake. Ask for Beaver."

The lake was blue and beautiful. Beaver was
sunning on the shore.

"Mr. Fox sent me—" began Rabbit.

"To look at my house," finished Beaver. He pointed
to it proudly. "I cut every log myself."

The house had a roof and walls. But something was
missing. "There are no windows or doors," Rabbit said.
"How do you get in?"

"I get into the house under water," Beaver explained. "Follow me and I'll show you." He dived into the lake with hardly a ripple.

But Rabbit stayed on dry land. "This won't do,"
he said. "I don't want to go swimming each time I
leave my house or come back. I'll have to talk to
Mr. Fox again."

But Mr. Fox said crossly, "I give you a house with a view, and you want a roof and walls. I give you a roof and walls, and now you want a door and a window."

Mr. Fox's clock struck the quarter-hour. It was almost lunchtime, and Mr. Fox was getting hungry. He looked at Rabbit and smiled a sly smile. "I know just the house for you," he said.

Mr. Fox led Rabbit down a long, winding path into the woods. At the end of the path was a stone house.

"As you can see," said Mr. Fox, "this house has everything—a roof, walls, a door, and a fine round window."

Pulling a key out of his pocket, Mr. Fox unlocked
the front door. He opened it wide. "After you," he said
politely to Rabbit.

Rabbit hopped into the house. Mr. Fox followed
him. The door closed tightly with a *click*.

"What about the view?" asked Rabbit.

"Let's look at the kitchen first," said Mr. Fox. "It's large and comfortable, and the stove is almost new."

On the iron stove stood a deep, shiny cooking pot. Mr. Fox lifted the lid. "Would you like to take a peek?" he asked.

Mr. Fox licked his lips and waited until Rabbit leaned over the pot. Then he grabbed for Rabbit with both paws!

But Rabbit was too quick for him! Springing away from the stove, Rabbit leaped straight through the fine round window of Mr. Fox's house.

Rabbit raced through the
woods as fast as he could.

He sped past the lake...

past Mrs. Robin's red mailbox...

and straight across Main Street.

Rabbit didn't stop hopping until he reached his own house. It looked very good to him now. It had a roof and walls and a strong front door. Rabbit dashed inside and locked the door behind him.

As he sank down on his bed to catch his breath,
Rabbit looked out the window. He saw the same
crooked pine tree. He saw the round, brown hill.

Rabbit had an idea. He stood up and pushed his bed around. He lay down again and looked out the window. Now he saw two tall oak trees and a round, green hill.

Rabbit was happy. His own house was the right house, after all.